THE BRASOV TABLATURE

RECENT RESEARCHES IN THE MUSIC OF THE BAROQUE ERA

Robert L. Marshall, general editor

A-R Editions, Inc., publishes six quarterly series—

Recent Researches in the Music of the Middle Ages and Early Renaissance,
Margaret Bent, general editor;

Recent Researches in the Music of the Renaissance,
James Haar and Howard Mayer Brown, general editors;

Recent Researches in the Music of the Baroque Era,
Robert L. Marshall, general editor;

Recent Researches in the Music of the Classical Era,
Eugene K. Wolf, general editor;

Recent Researches in the Music of the Nineteenth and Early Twentieth Centuries,
Rufus Hallmark, general editor;

Recent Researches in American Music,
H. Wiley Hitchcock, general editor—

which make public music that is being brought to light
in the course of current musicological research.

Each volume in the *Recent Researches* is devoted
to works by a single composer or to a single genre of composition,
chosen because of its potential interest to scholars and performers,
and prepared for publication according to the standards that govern
the making of all reliable historical editions.

Subscribers to this series, as well as patrons of subscribing institutions,
are invited to apply for information about the ''Copyright-Sharing Policy''
of A-R Editions, Inc., under which the contents of this volume
may be reproduced free of charge for study or performance.

Correspondence should be addressed:

A-R EDITIONS, INC.
315 West Gorham Street
Madison, Wisconsin 53703

RECENT RESEARCHES IN THE MUSIC OF THE BAROQUE ERA • VOLUME XL

THE BRASOV TABLATURE

(Brasov Music Manuscript 808): German Keyboard Studies 1680-1684

Edited by John H. Baron

A-R EDITIONS, INC. • MADISON

To Doris Ann

Labor, aspera difficilisve adeo res nulla reperta,
Assiduo qua non dicta labore foret.
Te, sine te ditare Deus, possetque tueri,
Vt tamen et praestes vult opus ipse tuum.

(Dedication, Brasov Music Manuscript 808, fol. 1ᵛ)

Copyright © 1982, A-R Editions, Inc.

ISSN 0484-0828

ISBN 0-89579-162-5

Library of Congress Cataloging in Publication Data:

Biblioteca Municipală Brasov. Manuscript. Music.
    The Brasov tablature.

    (Recent researches in the music of the baroque era ,
ISSN 0484-0828 ; v. 40)
    For organ, harpsichord, or clavichord.
    Edited from music ms. 808 in the Brasov City
Library.
    1. Keyboard music.   I. Baron, John H.
II. Title.   III. Series.
M2.R238   vol. 40 [M7]   82-13753
ISBN 0-89579-162-5

Contents

Preface

The Brasov Tablature is unusual in that it presents considerable information on the keyboard fingering technique of the late seventeenth century, and because it contains one of the earliest sets of preludes in successive keys (by Johann Heinrich Kittel).[1] This first modern transcription and printing of the Brasov manuscript makes it possible for students of baroque music to observe, first-hand, the performance practice of that time.

The Scribe and the Composers

Daniel Croner (1656–1740) was apparently a native of Kronstadt (now Brasov, Rumania). He began to copy the Brasov manuscript on 30 January 1681, while he lived in Bratislava; he completed it nearly four years later, on 20 November 1684.[2] Croner's aim seems to have been to copy what would be useful for his own keyboard playing, beginning with a set of etudes entitled *Applicaturae* (see p. xi) and continuing with typical works that he could employ during Lutheran services. Croner had entered theological school in the early 1680s and then devoted his life to his church. Although we do not know to what extent he may have used this tablature later on in his career, the manuscript demonstrates that even in his earlier years Croner had considerable knowledge of contemporary keyboard styles and forms.

Most of the composers whose works Croner copied are unknown. Croner may possibly have composed some of the anonymous pieces in the Brasov Tablature; however, these pieces do not seem to conform to Croner's style—compositionally they are much more interesting than the one work securely attributable to him (no. [84] in this edition). Johann Heinrich Kittel (1652–1682),[3] the composer of the twelve preludes in successive keys and of the "Capriccio on Brevem Bassum" in the tablature (nos. [1]–[13] in this edition), was court organist and music teacher to the children at the Dresden Electoral Court. Among Kittel's pupils was Johann Kuhnau, Bach's famous predecessor in Leipzig. Indeed, Kuhnau may have taken his idea of presenting preludes in successive keys in his two collections of 1689 and 1692 from Kittel; and J. S. Bach brought this type of presentation to its zenith a generation later. Two fugues in the Brasov Tablature (nos. [39] and [40]) are by Johann Ulich (1634–after 1687?), whom Croner cited in his manuscript as an organist in Wittenberg. Two additional fugues and a toccata in the tablature (nos. [49], [75], and [74], respectively) are by Bernhard Meyer (fl. ca. 1650), an organist in Zerbst.

The only famous composer represented in the Brasov Tablature is Johann Jakob Froberger (1616–1667), court organist to Emperor Ferdinand III in Vienna; what Croner calls a *"fuga* by Sign. Geor[*sic*] Frob." (no. [48]) is actually the final part of J. J. Froberger's "Toccata in D minor."[4]

The Source

The Brasov Tablature is one of two large keyboard manuscripts copied in German keyboard tablature by Daniel Croner. These manuscripts are now in the Brasov City Library. One of these manuscripts contains some 100 pieces and has the call number Mus. Ms. 948, mis. 5. The other manuscript, the Brasov Tablature, is the source of the transcriptions in the present edition; its call number is Mus. Ms. 808. The Brasov Tablature is in two sections, each with its own title page (see facsimile Plates I and II). Section I consists of seventy compositions: twenty-five pieces entitled either *praeludium* or *praeambulum*; thirty entitled *fuga*; six toccatas; five verses of a Magnificat; a fantasia; a principium; and a concordantiae. In addition, Section I begins with the *Applicaturae*, discussed below (see Performance Suggestions) and ends with an index of the pieces according to tone. Section II is comprised of the thirteen works by Johann Heinrich Kittel—twelve preludes in successive keys and a capriccio—and the single fugue by Croner himself.

Although all the pieces contained in the Brasov Tablature are transcribed in the present edition, these works do not appear here in the same order as they do in the source. The Table *Complete Contents of Brasov Music Manuscript* gives the original order of the entire source manuscript. Original titles are also reproduced in the Table. Except for the internal order of the Kittel preludes, the placement of pieces in the source seems arbitrary. Therefore, although they do not appear until Section II of the manuscript, the pieces by Kittel are presented as the first thirteen works in this edition because of their historical importance (in the case of nos. [1]–[12]) as one of the earliest sets of preludes in successive keys. Kittel's capriccio follows the twelve preludes both in the source and in this edition; these thirteen pieces appear here in their original internal order because together they form a unit. The rest of the pieces from the Brasov Tablature have been grouped into categories and are presented in this edition as follows: the concordantiae (no. [14]); preludes (nos. [15–33]); fugues (nos. [34–50]); pieces whose titles assign them false genres in that they are fugues that are labeled *"praeludium"* (nos. [51–56]) or preludes that are labeled *"fuga"* ([57–68]); toccatas (nos. [69–74]); an isolated fugue (no. [75]) that, because it is by Bernhard Meyer and because it is of the third mode, we believe is intended to follow Meyer's "Toccata of the third tone" (no. [74]); the fantasia and principium (nos. [76] and [77]); and the settings of the Magnificat verses (nos. [78–83]). The final piece (no. [84]), both in this edition and in the manuscript source, is a fugue by Croner himself, and it is thus an appropriate close to the edition.

Table: Complete Contents of Brasov Music Manuscript

Piece No.	Source Location (fol.)	Title or Description in Source
	1	[title page (see Plate I)]
	1ᵛ	[poem (see page iv)]
	2–3ᵛ	Applicaturae
[15]	3ᵛ–4	Praeambulum supra Ich ruff zu dir H. Jesu Christ
[53]	4ᵛ–5	Praeludium ex E
[17]	4ᵛ–5	Praeambulum: ex D
[16]	5ᵛ–6	Praeamb: ex C
[18]	5ᵛ–6	Praeamb: ex A
[19]	6ᵛ–7	Praeambu: ex A
[23]	6ᵛ–7	Praelud: ex F
[76]	7ᵛ–9	Fantasia ex G
[70]	8ᵛ–9	Tocata in G
[38]	9ᵛ–11	Fuga ex D
[41]	10ᵛ–12	Fuga ex C
[42]	11ᵛ–13	Fuga ex G
[72]	12ᵛ–15	Tocata ex E
[60]	14ᵛ–15	Fuga in G
[66]	15ᵛ–16	Fuga in G Die 1. Febr.
[69]	15ᵛ–17	Tocata ex D
[21]	16ᵛ–17	Praelud: ex G
[52]	16ᵛ–17	Praelud: ex G♭
[54]	17ᵛ–18	Praeludi: ex G♭
[20]	17ᵛ–18	Praeludi: ex A
[50]	17ᵛ–19	Fuga ex A
[67]	18ᵛ–19	Fuga ex D
[56]	19ᵛ–20	Praeludi: ex E
[77]	19ᵛ–20	Principium ex G♮ . 8. toni
[43]	20ᵛ–21	Fuga in F
[61]	21ᵛ–22ᵛ	Fuga ex D
[64]	22ᵛ–23	Fuga Aolij ex A
[44]	23ᵛ–24	Fuga in A
[22]	23ᵛ–24	Praelu: ex G
[73]	24ᵛ–26	Tocata 2di Toni in G
[47]	25ᵛ–27ᵛ	Fuga 2di Toni ex G
[14]	27ᵛ–28	Concordantiae ex C
[46]	27ᵛ–29	Fuga in G
[65]	28ᵛ–29	Fuga 2di Toni ex D♮
[25]	28ᵛ–29ᵛ	Praeludi: 4ti Toni ex E
[24]	29ᵛ–30	Praelud: 6. Toni ex F
[29]	29ᵛ–30	Praeamb: 7. et 8. Toni Per 2dam transponi in A♮
[45]	30ᵛ–31	Fuga ex G
[27]	31ᵛ–32	Praelud: 1. et 2. To: in G. Die 2. Febr:
[32]	31ᵛ–32	Praeamb: 11. et 12. Toni ex C
[59]	32ᵛ–33	Fuga 3. et 4. To. ex A♮
[62]	32ᵛ–33	Fuga 7. et 8. To: ex C
[33]	33ᵛ–34	Praeludi: 5. et 6. Toni ex B
[57]	33ᵛ–34	Fuga 9. et 10 To: ex D
[31]	34ᵛ–35	Praeludi: 11. et 12. To: ex F
[28]	34ᵛ–35	Praeamb: 11. et 12. Toni ex D♮
[30]	35ᵛ–36	Praeamb: 9. et 10. Ton: ex A
[26]	35ᵛ–36	Praeamb: 7. et 8. Ton. ex G♮
[34]	36ᵛ–38	Fuga Super Ach wie sehnlich: ex G
[37]	37ᵛ–38	Fuga ex D
[78]	38ᵛ–39	Intonatio Magnificat. 4. Toni. ex E
[79]	39ᵛ–40	Magnificat 8. Toni. 1. Versus ex G
[80]	40ᵛ–41	Secundus Versus, Coral in Discant mit 2. Clavierung in G
[81]	41ᵛ–42	Tertius Versus inb. G
[82]	42ᵛ–43	Quintus Versus im Bass Coral. in G
[83]	42ᵛ–44	Sextus Versus Tutti.
[58]	43ᵛ–44	Fuga ex D
[35]	44ᵛ–45	Fuga. Supra Was mein Gott will. ex A
[71]	45ᵛ–46	Tocata ex C. Die 5. Febr.
[51]	46ᵛ–47	Praelud: ex G
[68]	46ᵛ–47	Fuga ex G
[39]	47ᵛ–48	Fuga ex C supra Allein zu Dir Herr. Auth. Jo. Ul: Org. Witteb.
[40]	47ᵛ–48	Fuga ex E. Supra Erbarm dich mein o H: Gott. Auth: Joh. Ulich
[63]	47ᵛ–48	Fuga ex D
[36]	48ᵛ–50	Fuga vel Variatio ex F. Super Wo Gott zum Hauss nicht graben
[48]	49ᵛ–50	Fuga di Sign: Geor. Frob:
[74]	50ᵛ–52	Toccata 3tii Toni durch Mordantam. B. Meyer. [at the end] Folget die Fuga drauf.
[75]	52ᵛ–55	Fuga Simplex Tertii Modi B. Meyer
[49]	54ᵛ–56	Fuga ex A. B. Meyer.
[55]	55ᵛ–56ᵛ	Praeludium ex E
	57–57ᵛ	Index Fugarum, Praeludiorum et Tocatarum, juxta ordinem Tonorum positus ut: ex C, D, E, F, G, A, B.
	58	[title page (see Plate II)]
[1]	58ᵛ–59	Folgen Numr 12. Praeamb. durch alle Claves auf clavichordien und Instrum: zu gebrauchen. Praeamb: ex C♭ moll

Piece No.	Source Location (fol.)	Title or Description in Source
[2]	59ᵛ–61	Praeludium ex C♮
[3]	61ᵛ–65	Praeamb: ex D♭
[4]	64ᵛ–69	Praeludium ex D♮
[5]	68ᵛ–72	Praeamb: ex E
[6]	71ᵛ–74	Praelud: ex F
[7]	73ᵛ–75	Praeamb: ex G♭
[8]	75ᵛ–78	Praelud: ex G♮
[9]	77ᵛ–80	Praeamb: ex A♭
[10]	80ᵛ–82	Praeludium ex A♮
[11]	81ᵛ–83	Praeamb: ex B
[12]	83ᵛ–86	Praeludium ex H
[13]	85ᵛ–88	Capriccio supra Brevem Bassum b a g f [e♭] d c f
[84]	87ᵛ–91	Fuga ex E. Dan: Cron: Ao: 84. d. 20. Nov.

The Music

During the second half of the seventeenth century, German keyboard music reached a level of perfection and a degree of innovation never before realized. A large number of composers contributed to the evolution of certain secular and sacred forms and styles that were brought to their highest point of development a generation later in the works of J. S. Bach. The church music, based on Dutch and Italian models but incorporating many North German Lutheran traits, is utilitarian and was composed in the following forms: preludes; fugues and toccatas for opening and closing services; chorale settings for accompanying or introducing congregational singing of chorales; and organ Magnificats for Vespers services. The secular music of this time was largely confined to dance movements that are grouped into suites. Such suites, however, were not intended to accompany dancing; rather, they were meant for the enjoyment of the performer only. Pedagogical works, composed for the training of younger organists and harpsichordists, were simply written in the same genres of composition employed in the church service or in secular situations. Although the art of improvisation was highly cultivated in keyboard music of this period, any improvising that was done was based on the student's knowledge of the rules and traditions of written preludes, fugues, toccatas, and other such pieces. Although some of the works in the Brasov Tablature demonstrate certain innovative trends of the times, Kittel's thirteen harpsichord or clavichord pieces and the other seventy-one pieces (some for harpsichord and some for organ) in the manuscript are a part of the late-seventeenth-century German tradition of utilitarian keyboard music.

The Kittel Preludes and Capriccio

The twelve preludes by Kittel appear to be the earliest known keyboard preludes in successive keys (C minor, C major, D minor, D major, E mixed minor and major, F major, G minor, G major, A minor, A major, B-flat major, and B minor). Although the composers generally regarded as the first to arrange individual suites or preludes in a determined order of tonalities are Johann Pachelbel and Johann Kuhnau, their collections appeared after Kittel's, which we know was copied into the Brasov Tablature in 1682 (see Plate II). The earliest known source for Pachelbel's suites is a manuscript dated 1683.[5] We cannot absolutely establish the priority of the composition of Kittel's work over Pachelbel's, however, since both Kittel's and Pachelbel's suites may have been written several years before being copied into their respective manuscripts. Kuhnau's *partien* with introductory *praeludia* were first issued in 1689 (the major keys) and 1692 (the minor keys).[6] Indeed, it is possible that Kuhnau received the idea for his collection from Kittel, who was his teacher (see above). There is no musical connection between Kittel's and Kuhnau's works, other than the concept of preludes in successive keys, just as there is none between Kittel's and the preludes and fugues of J. F. K. Fischer[7] and of Bach; although Kittel's preludes share with Bach's *Well-Tempered Clavier* preludes a seemingly didactic purpose.

Each of the Kittel preludes is a short piece of between ten and forty-one measures in length. As is typical of baroque preludes, each of Kittel's pieces is in one section, and there is no formal internal repetition. A single rhythmic idea dominates each piece, and the single melodic motive in each is usually (but not always) a short arpeggio. The harmony is solid, with ample variety of chords (not at all confined to tonic and dominant), and although there is no modulation, secondary dominants are judiciously scattered about. Kittel's capriccio (no. [13]) is a set of twelve variations over a two-measure ground bass. Although a few of the variations include arpeggios, Kittel employs more scalar motives here than in the preludes.

Other Pieces in the Brasov Tablature

The remaining preludes in the Brasov Tablature are short works that often have runs and other figurations and that do not strictly maintain horizontal voice lines. Most of the pieces labeled *"praeludium"* or *"praeambulum"* fit this description, as do some of the pieces labeled *"fuga"* (i.e., nos. [57]-[68]; see above under The Source).

Fugues in the Brasov Tablature often begin with the traditional canzona rhythm (♩ ♪♪ | o), exhibit fairly strict imitation, and maintain horizontal voice lines. However, none of these pieces is a strict fugue in the eighteenth-century sense: some are interrupted by runs (e.g., nos. [38] and [41]), and in others (e.g., no. [50]), the linear identity of voices is obscured. These characteristics are found in most of the pieces labeled *"fuga"* and in some of those labeled *"praeludium"* (i.e., nos. [51-56]; see above under The Source). Of special interest are the six fugues based on chorales. In "Praeambulum supra 'Ich ruff zu Dir, Herr Jesu Christ' " (no. [15]), the complete chorale melody is presented without interruption, alteration, or figuration in the right hand (fermatas indicate the phrase endings of the chorale); the left hand has a single line of counterpoint in faster note values that paraphrases and often anticipates each chorale phrase. Unlike no. [15], the two chorale fugues by Ulich (nos. [39] and [40]) each use only the opening phrase of their respective chorales as the subject of a short, imitative piece in which all voices move at the same speed. The first, based on "Allein zu Dir, Herr Jesu Christ" (no. [39]), has four voice lines; however, from m. 12 to the end, the piece becomes more chordal than contrapuntal, and extra voices are added in the last two measures. The second, "Erbarm dich mein o Herre Gott" (no. [40]), maintains a strict three-voice texture until the last measure, where two extra notes are added. The anonymous "Fuga Super 'Ach wie sehnlich' " (no. [34]) is a much more substantial fugue in four voices (except for a few added notes near the end). The entire chorale is utilized motivically in this piece rather than being presented as a *cantus firmus* in any one voice. Phrase two of the chorale serves as countersubject to phrase one as subject. The "Fuga Supra 'Was mein Gott will' "(no. [35]) is a large fugue that is based exclusively on the first phrase of its chorale. The organ fugue on "Wo Gott zum Haus nicht graben" (no. [36]) first presents the complete chorale once in the right hand; this statement is made in long notes and each phrase is marked by a fermata at its end and separated from the others by rests. The chorale melody then is given in the pedal in the second half of the piece. The left hand provides continual imitation and counterpoint in the first section, and the right does the same once the pedal enters.

The Concordantiae (no. [14]) is a chordal piece with simple elaboration by running eighth-notes, while the Principium (no. [77]) is a hybrid of chords with runs and, at the beginning, four-voice counterpoint with imitation.[8] Each of the Toccatas (nos. [69]-[74]) is a chordal work with elaboration by such figurations as running eighth- and sixteenth-notes, scalar passages, repeated rhythmic motives, and mordents. The "Toccata in G" (no. [70]) is unique among these pieces in that it begins with contrapuntal, imitative entries of three voices, before it reaches elaborated chords.

The Magnificat pieces (nos. [78]–[83]) form a group that is based on a *cantus firmus* drawn from traditional chant;[9] however, this group does not provide music for all ten verses of the Vespers Canticle, nor does it give the two verses of the Lesser Doxology that always follow in this canticle. In performing Magnificats in the seventeenth century, alternation of organ verses with sung chant was common. Here the performance probably was as follows: organ intonation (no. [78]); organ performance of verses 1–3 and 5–6 (nos. [79]–[83]); and sung performance of verses 4, 7–10, and the Lesser Doxology. In all but one Magnificat verse set in this tablature (no. [81]), the *cantus firmus* is presented in long notes in the organ pedal, while the two hands usually provide contrapuntal accompaniment that includes frequent imitation.

The pieces in the Brasov collection are unpretentious, and they conform to the simple norms established in the other German keyboard tablatures of the time. The forms, textures, styles, and harmonies are typical of the pre-Bach era. The most striking characteristic of some of the pieces in the Brasov Tablature is the dissonance created by the apparent cross-relations and chromaticism. Such dissonance is especially evident in nos. [27], [30], [38], [40], and [73]; yet this occurs within a context of clear harmonic direction, and the dissonance becomes simply an ornament. The charm of all of the works in the collection lies in their ingenuousness.

Performance Suggestions

According to the title page of Section II of the source (see Plate II), Kittel's thirteen pieces are to be performed on a clavichord or spinet (harpsichord)—"auff Clavichordien und Spinetten zu gebrauchen." The other pieces of the Brasov Tablature generally seem to be best suited to the organ. (Nos. [26], [34], [37], and five of the six Magnificat verse settings, in particular, must be performed on an organ with pedal.) In some cases where there are voice-crossings and unisons, a two-manual instrument is preferable.

The six anonymous *Applicaturae* (see below) that appear at the beginning of the source manuscript and the thirteen pieces by Kittel (nos. [1]–[13]) that are presented near the end of the source all have indicated fingerings. In right-hand ascending scales, the basic patterns show fingers 3 and 4 for nearly every note,[10] with 3 shifting over 4. In descending right-hand scales, 3 shifts over 2. There is more variety in left-hand scales: in ascending left-hand scales, Croner, or the source he copied, seems to have changed his method from 2 over 1 in the *Applicaturae* to 4 over 3 and 4 over 2 in the Kittel pieces. It is obvious that Kittel (or Croner) shunned the right-hand thumb and left-hand little finger as much as possible, though in some octave leaps and chords, they cannot be avoided. Avoidance of these fingerings probably stemmed from the

Applicaturae

1. Applicatur der rechten Hand zum herunter lauffen (Fingering of the right hand going down)

2. Applicatur der rechten Hand zum hinauff lauffen (Fingering of the right hand going up)

3. Applicatur der lincken Hand zum herunter lauffen (Fingering of the left hand going down)

4. Applicatur der lincken Hand zum hinauff lauffen (Fingering of the left hand going up)

5. Noch ein andere Applicatur der Fingern zum hinauff lauffen (Still another fingering going up)

6. Applicatur zum hinunter lauffen (Fingering going down)

Kurtzer Unterricht der Application auff Instrumenten, zum Vnter v. hinauff lauffen, in beyden Händen.
Geschrieben zu Breslau im Febr. 1680. Die 31. Januar.
(Short instruction on instrumental fingering for both hands going up and down.
Written in Breslau in February, 1680. [Today is] January 31 [1681].) [11]

fact that the performer did not sit squarely in front of the keyboard as in modern performance, but, instead, sat at an angle where the right shoulder was nearer the keyboard than the left shoulder.

There are two ornaments used by Croner in the Brasov Tablature. The mordent ⁀ can be interpreted as follows:[12]

Ex. 1.

Fingering for this ornament seems to be 1 and 2 or 2 and 3 in those pieces for which the manuscript indicates fingering. The sign + can be interpreted in several ways, one of which is as the equivalent of the mordent ⁀ . Another possibility is as an appoggiatura:

Ex. 2.

Other possibilities seem less likely in a tablature of this period and provenance.

The Edition

This edition is based exclusively on the manuscript copied by Daniel Croner (Brasov Music Manuscript 808). The source manuscript is clearly notated in German keyboard tablature. Because, as is typical of keyboard tablatures, none of the pieces has a key signature in the source, all such signatures have been supplied editorially here. These signatures are supplied to avoid excessive use of sharp and flat symbols within the score and to relate the pieces to modern notation. To supply key signatures, the editor has considered the title of each work as given in the source (see pp. viii-ix). These titles often indicate major or minor tonality by means of a ♭ or ♮ sign placed next to the "key" letter (e.g., A♮ in a title indicates a piece in A major, while A♭ indicates a piece in A minor). However, there are also pieces in the tablature whose titles bear no such indications, and for these works, the editor has taken into account the beginning and ending tonalities (with consideration of such cadential alterations as Picardy thirds) and the use of accidentals within each piece. Indeed, the titles as given in the source are faithfully reproduced in this edition even when such titles seem to be at variance with the tonalities that are actually expressed in the piece (e.g., in no. [38]). Application of key signatures has resulted in the editorial elimination of accidentals that, although they are given in the source, are now implied by the presence of the signature. The editor has retained only those tablature accidentals that (1) cancel the new signature, (2) are needed for cautionary purposes, or (3) return the original accidental after a previous cancel-

lation. Since all accidentals are unambiguously notated in the source (e.g., B in the tablature is our customary b-flat, H is our customary b, ⅍ is either d-sharp or e-flat), all cross-relations and other "wrong sounds" have been allowed to stand, and the rules of *musica ficta* have not been applied here. Octave position is indicated clearly in the source (c̄ = middle c; h = b a half-step below middle c; c = c an octave below middle c; C = c two octaves below middle c; and c̿ = c an octave above middle c). Obvious errors in the source are corrected in this edition, however, and such corrections are enclosed in square brackets and documented in the Critical Notes. Cautionary accidentals in parentheses have been added by the editor (e.g., p. 8, m. 23). Rhythm is usually indicated precisely in the source; all pieces are assumed to be in $\frac{4}{4}$ unless another meter sign is given, and only once is a tempo designation given (see no. [9]).

The fingerings for nos. [1]–[13] are transcribed in the edition just as they appear in the manuscript, with the following exceptions: (1) In chords for which not all the fingering is indicated in the manuscript, a dash has been added where necessary to clarify to which note the fingering applies. (2) Fingering has been added in nos. [5] and [7]; such editorial fingering indications are given in square brackets. (3) Parentheses are placed around the fingering of measures 20–21 in no. [13]; even though these fingerings do not seem to make sense, they are exactly what appear in the source manuscript.

Critical Notes

The Critical Notes below document discrepancies between the present edition and the Brasov Tablature. Pitches are given according to the usual method, wherein middle c = c′; the c above middle c = c′′, and so forth.

[3] Praeambulum in D Minor

M. 30, R.H., upper voice, notes 1–4 are one octave higher. M. 31, R.H., upper voice, notes 1–4 are one octave higher.

[5] Praeambulum in E

M. 5, R.H., note 2 is one octave lower. M. 7, R.H., note 1 is one octave lower. M. 8, L.H., fingering for notes 10-12 is 5 1 2. M. 17, R.H., notes 2 and 5 are each one octave lower.

[6] Praeludium in F

M. 9, L.H., note 2 is one octave lower.

[7] Praeambulum in G Minor

M. 3, L.H., note 1 is c. M. 11, L.H., note 3, fingering mark for this note is obscured.

[9] *Praeambulum in A Minor*

The source has the notes of the first and last measures grouped as though they are in $\frac{4}{4}$, and the rest of the notes in the remaining mm. are grouped as though they are in $\frac{6}{4}$.

[13] *Capriccio on Brevem Bassum*

M. 19, the parentheses in this m. appear in the source; perhaps the chord in this m. is suggested as a final chord if the piece is to be terminated after variation IX. Mm. 20–21, R.H., the fingering in these mm. makes no sense unless Kittel [or Croner] designed this passage as an exercise in which the hand is expected to jump a great deal. Mm. 25–26, the piece ends at m. 25; m. 26 is suggested editorially and is supplied here by analogy with m. 19.

[14] *Concordantiae in C*

M. 18, an extra m. appears after this one in the source; it contains two whole-notes aligned vertically (c and c'').

[15] *Praeambulum on "Ich ruff zu Dir, Herr Jesu Christ"*

The chorale melody is used by J.S. Bach in his *Cantata 177*.

[16] *Praeambulum in C*

M. 12, L.H., upper voice, notes 3 and 4 are sixteenth-notes.

[19] *Praeambulum in A*

M. 5, L.H., upper voice, notes 1 and 2 are one octave lower. M. 7, L.H., note 1 is one octave higher.

[22] *Praeludium in G*

M. 2, L.H., final note is one octave lower.

[25] *Praeludium of the fourth tone in E*

M. 10, R.H., notes 1-4 are sixteenth-notes.

[26] *Praeambulum of the seventh and eighth tones in G Major*

M. 13, L.H., upper voice, final note is one octave lower. Mm. 14-18, pedal line is omitted; added here by analogy with L.H. lower voice in order to smooth over the awkward L.H. of m. 16.

[27] *Praeludium of the first and second tones in G "February Second"*

M. 10, R.H., lower voice, final note is a quarter-note.

[29] *Praeambulum of the seventh and eighth tones transposed to A Major*

M. 5, R.H., lower voice, note 4 is a half-note.

[30] *Praeambulum of the ninth and tenth tones in A*

M. 13, L.H., upper voice, note 1 does not appear in the source.

[31] *Praeludium of the eleventh and twelfth tones in F*

M. 1, R.H., lower voice, note 3 is an eighth-note.

[32] *Praeambulum of the eleventh and twelfth tones in C*

M. 10, R.H., upper voice, beats 3 and 4, rhythm is unclear.

[33] *Praeludium of the fifth and sixth tones in B-flat*

M. 10, L.H., upper voice, penultimate note is one octave lower. M. 18, R.H., lower voice, last note is one octave lower.

[35] *Fuga in A on "Was mein Gott will"*

The chorale melody is used by J. S. Bach in *Cantata 103*. M. 19, R.H., lower part, notes 1–4 are one octave lower. Mm. 41–43, R.H., upper part does not appear in the source.

[37] *Fuga in D*

Mm. 23–24, L.H., lower part does not appear in the source.

[38] *Fuga in D*

M. 25, L.H., note 1 omitted; supplied here in order to complete the phrase.

[39] *Fuga in C on "Allein zu Dir, Herr Jesu Christ"*

The chorale melody is used by J. S. Bach in *Cantata 33*.

[43] *Fuga in F*

M. 24, R.H., rest 1 is an eighth-rest and notes 2–4 are eighth-notes.

[44] *Fuga in A*

M. 33, L.H., upper voice, note 1 omitted; supplied here in order to complete the phrase.

[45] *Fuga in G*

M. 8, R.H., note 7 is an eighth-note, and notes 8–13 are sixteenth-notes.

[46] *Fuga in G*

M. 3, R.H., notes 6 and 7 are eighth-notes. M. 14, L.H., lower voice, note 1 is a dotted quarter. Mm. 24–27, R.H., upper voice written one octave higher. M. 25, R.H., note 1 is an eighth-note. Mm. 25–27, R.H., lower voice is written one octave higher.

[47] *Fuga of the second tone in G*

M. 8, L.H., note 1 is omitted; supplied here to correct rhythm. M. 14, R.H., note 1 is f'-sharp.

[48] *Fuga*

M. 4, R.H., upper voice, note 1 is an octave lower.

[49] *Fuga in A*

M. 9, beats 3 and 4, R.H., lower voice, and L.H., upper voice, are reversed.

[50] *Fuga in A*

M. 2, L.H., note 1 is a half-note.

[51] *Praeludium in G*

M. 7, R.H., lower voice written one octave lower.

[54] *Praeludium in G Minor*

M. 16, R.H., lower voice part is unclear.

[56] *Praeludium in E*

M. 5, R.H., beats 1 and 2, upper and lower voices are exchanged for one another.

[57] *Fuga of the ninth and tenth tones in D*

M. 6, R.H., lower voice, and L.H., upper voice, are reversed. M. 7, L.H., whole-rest added below notation (i.e., letters in tablature).

[59] *Fuga of the third and fourth tones in A Major*

M. 3, R.H., lower voice, note 3 is an eighth-note. M. 4, R.H., upper voice, note 1 is sharped. M. 12, L.H., upper voice, notes 1–4 are sixteenths.

[61] *Fuga in D*

M. 16, L.H., note 7 is f-natural.

[62] *Fuga of the seventh and eighth tones in C*

M. 13, L.H., note 8 is one octave lower.

[65] *Fuga of the second tone in D Major*

M. 13, R.H., lower voices written one octave lower; upper voice and raised lower voices supplied here in order to complete R.H. phrase.

[66] *Fuga in G for February 1*

M. 10, R.H., last two notes are eighths. M. 11, R.H., chord on beats 3 and 4 written under a fermata, and ties are omitted. M. 12, R.H., chord omitted; supplied here by sustaining from m. 11.

[67] *Fuga in D*

Cross-relations in this piece reflect the source exactly.

[71] *Toccata in C: "the fifth of February"*

M. 18, R.H., lower voice is one octave higher.

[78] *Magnificat: Intonation of the fourth tone in E*

M. 5, R.H., upper voice, note 4 is an eighth-note. M. 24, R.H., upper voice is one octave lower in this m. M. 29, beats 2 and 3 are unclear rhythmically.

[79] *Magnificat: Verse 1 of the eighth tone in G*

Mm. 19 and 22, R.H., lower voice is one octave lower in these mm. M. 36, L.H., notes 2, 6, and 8 are one octave higher; Pedal, whole-rest replaced by 2 half-notes (B, B).

[80] *Magnificat: Verse 2 in G*

M. 10, R.H., lower voice is one octave higher in this m.

[81] *Magnificat: Verse 3 in G*

M. 10, L.H., note 1 is one octave higher. M. 12, L.H., note 1 is one octave lower. M. 31, R.H., upper voice, rhythm is unclear. M. 32, L.H., upper voice, note 1 is a quarter-note.

[83] *Magnificat: Verse 6*

M. 31, R.H., lower voice omitted; supplied here by repeating tone from m. 30.

[84] *Fuga in E*

Mm. 14 and 22, L.H., lower voice, notes 1 and 2 are linked by a tie.

Acknowledgments

In 1963, a photocopy of the Brasov Tablature was made available to me through the kind offices of the Hon. Henry S. Reuss, U.S. House of Representatives, and Mr. William A. Bell, Cultural Affairs Officer of the American Legation in Bucharest. The staff of A-R Editions, Inc., have made invaluable suggestions for the improvement of the prefatory material and have been most helpful in the preparation and presentation of this volume.

John H. Baron
Newcomb College
March 1982   Tulane University

Notes

1. For a fuller discussion of the importance of the Brasov Tablature, see John H. Baron, "A 17th-Century Keyboard Tablature in Brasov," *Journal of the American Musicological Society* XX (1967): 279–285.

2. Croner provided this information on the title page of the manuscript source (see Plate I) and in his heading for the last piece of the source (no. [84]).

3. In citing Kittel on the manuscript's title page, Croner seems to have confused Kittel's middle name with that of the latter's patron, the Elector Johann Georg (see Plate II). Cf. Baron, "A 17th-Century Keyboard Tablature," p. 283.

4. See Froberger's works, edited by G. Adler, *Denkmäler der Tonkunst in Österreich*, X/2: 19–21. I am grateful to Joshua Rifkin for pointing this out (communication from J. Rifkin, *Journal of the American Musicological Society* XII [1969]: 142).

5. They are printed from a manuscript dated 1683 in J. Pachelbel, *Klavierwerke*, ed. Max Seiffert, *Denkmäler Deutscher Tonkunst*, II/2 (Leipzig: 1901): 62-105, xxvi and xxxiii-xxxiv.

6. Johann Kuhnau, *Klavierübung* (2 vols.; Leipzig, 1689 and 1692), ed. Karl Päsler; rev. H.J. Moser, *Denkmäler Deutscher Tonkunst*, I/4 (Graz, 1958).

7. *Ariadne Musica* (1715), in *Sämtliche Werke*, ed. Ernst. V. Werra (Leipzig, 1901), pp. 75-93.

8. The term "*principium*" may be derived from Cicero's designation of the introduction to a speech as *Principium*; this term could be applied to an instrumental introduction to a vocal piece. See Warren Kirkendale, "Ciceronians versus Aristotelians on the Ricercar as Exordium, from Bembo to Bach," *Journal of the American Musicological Society* XXXII (1979): 21–28, 41.

9. All the verses except the Intonation (no. [78]) are based on the Gregorian Chant Magnificat of the Eighth Tone; the Intonation is based on the fourth Magnificat Tone; but the opening note is an addition to the original chant.

10. Croner considers the thumb of each hand to be 1 and the little finger of each hand to be 5.

11. In *Applicatur* 6, the first chord in the left hand probably should have the lower note up an octave, and the right-hand fingering probably should be 4 2 3 4 instead of 4 3 2 4.

12. These ornaments are based on Robert Donington, *The Interpretation of Early Music* (London: Faber and Faber, 1963), pp. 572–573 and Chapter XXI.

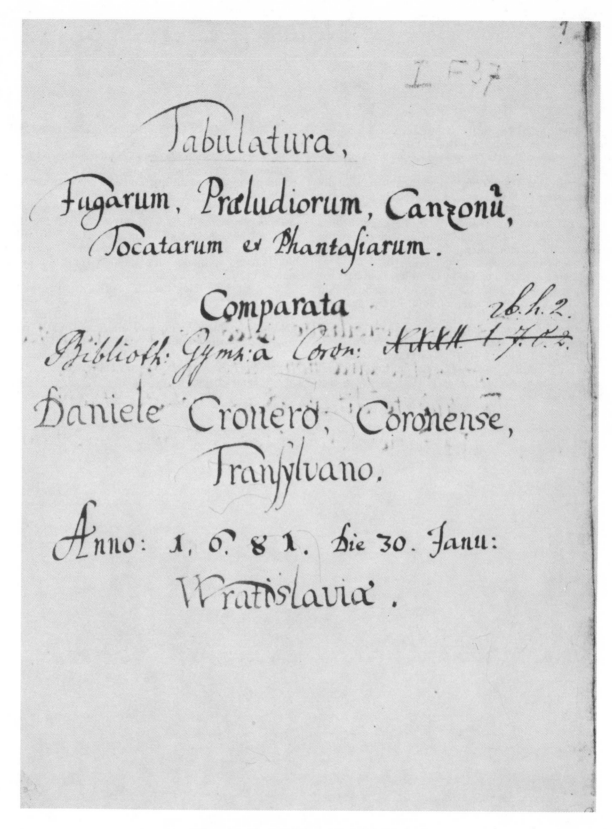

Plate I.   Brasov Mus. Ms. 808, fol. 1.
(Courtesy, Kronstadt Gymnasium Library; shelf no. I F 37)
The title page to Section I on fol. 1 is translated as follows:
Tablature of fugues, preludes, canzonas, toccatas and fantasias. Collected by Daniel Croner, native of
Kronstadt, Transylvania. January 30, 1681: in Bratislava.

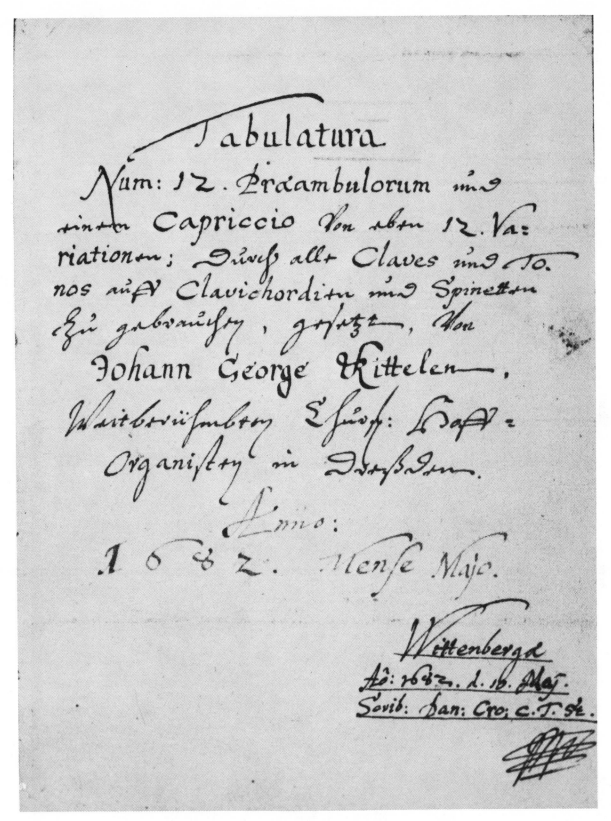

Plate II.   Brasov Mus. Ms. 808, fol. 58.
(Courtesy, Kronstadt Gymnasium Library; shelf no. I F 37)
The title page to Section II on fol. 58 is translated as follows:
Tablature numbering 12 praeambulums with a capriccio also with 12 variations; to be used through all the keys
and modes on the clavichord and spinet, composed by Johann George Kittel, famous organist of the
Electoral Court in Dresden. May 1682. Wittenberg, May 10, 1682,
scribe Daniel Croner, C. T. St. [?Kronstadt theology student].

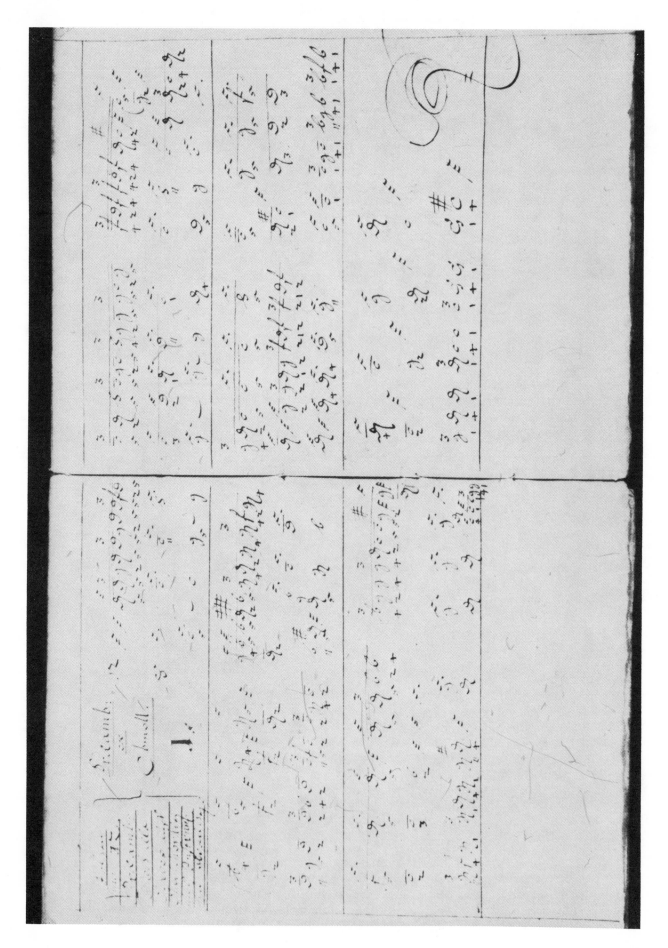

Plate III.　Brasov Mus. Ms. 808, fols. 58ᵛ-59.
(Courtesy, Kronstadt Gymnasium Library; shelf no. I F 37)

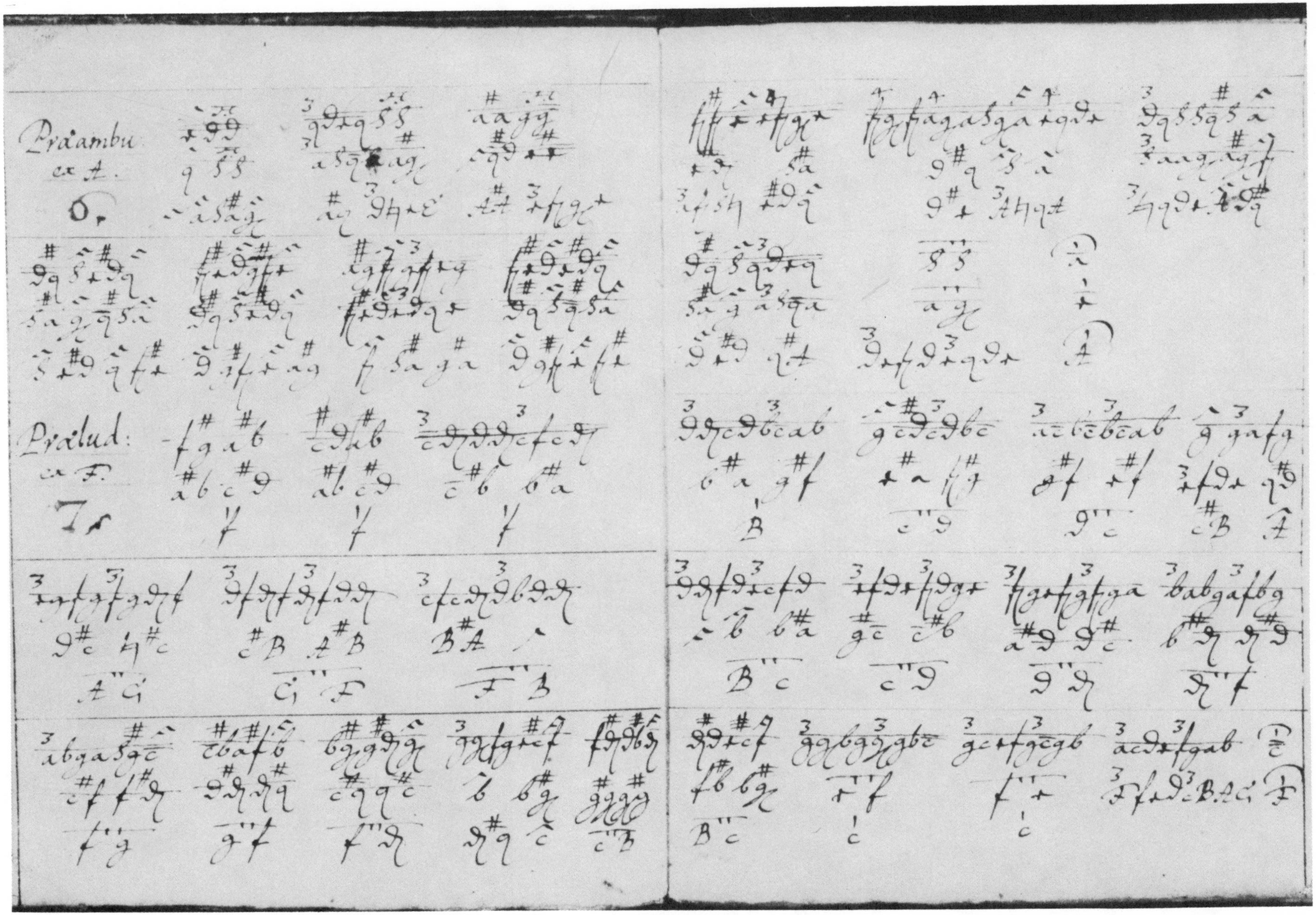

Plate IV. Brasov Mus. Ms. 808, fols. 6ᵛ-7.
(Courtesy, Kronstadt Gymnasium Library: shelf no. I F 37)

THE BRASOV TABLATURE

[1] Praeambulum in C Minor

Johann Heinrich Kittel

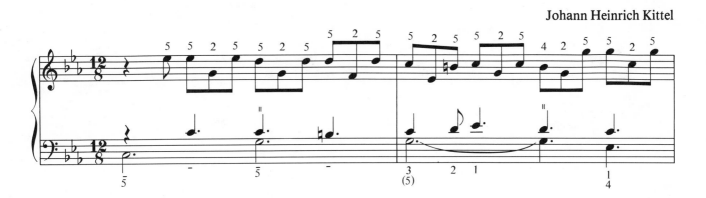

2

[2] Praeludium in C Major

Johann Heinrich Kittel

[3] Praeambulum in D Minor

Johann Heinrich Kittel

[4] Praeludium in D Major

Johann Heinrich Kittel

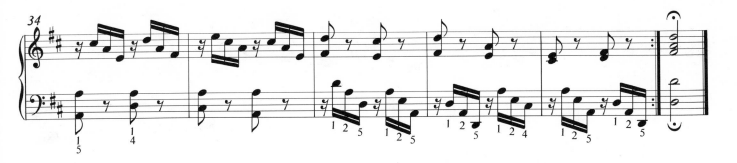

[5] Praeambulum in E

Johann Heinrich Kittel

[6] Praeludium in F

Johann Heinrich Kittel

[7] Praeambulum in G Minor

Johann Heinrich Kittel

[8] Praeludium in G Major

Johann Heinrich Kittel

[9] Praeambulum in A Minor

Allegro

Johann Heinrich Kittel

[10] Praeludium in A Major

Johann Heinrich Kittel

[11] Praeambulum in B-flat

Johann Heinrich Kittel

[12] Praeludium in B

Johann Heinrich Kittel

[13] Capriccio on Brevem Bassum

Johann Heinrich Kittel

[14] Concordantiae in C

16

[15] Praeambulum on ''Ich ruff zu Dir, Herr Jesu Christ''

[16] Praeambulum in C

[17] Praeambulum in D

[18] Praeambulum in A

[19] Praeambulum in A

[20] Praeludium in A

[21] Praeludium in G

[22] Praeludium in G

[23] Praeludium in F

[24] Praeludium of the sixth tone in F

[25] Praeludium of the fourth tone in E

[26] Praeambulum of the seventh and eighth tones in G Major

Pedal

[27] Praeludium of the first and second tones in G
"February Second"

[28] Praeambulum of the eleventh and twelfth tones in D Major

[29] Praeambulum of the seventh
and eighth tones transposed to A Major

[30] Praeambulum of the ninth and tenth tones in A

[31] Praeludium of the eleventh and twelfth tones in F

[32] Praeambulum of the eleventh and twelfth tones in C

[33] Praeludium of the fifth and sixth tones in B-flat

[34] Fuga in G on ''Ach wie sehnlich''

[35] Fuga in A on ''Was mein Gott will''

[36] Fuga or Variation in F on
"Wo Gott zum Haus nicht graben"

[37] Fuga in D

[38] Fuga in D

[39] Fuga in C on ''Allein zu Dir,
Herr Jesu Christ''

Johann Ulich

38

[40] Fuga in E on ''Erbarm dich mein o Herre Gott''

Johann Ulich

[41] Fuga in C

[42] Fuga in G

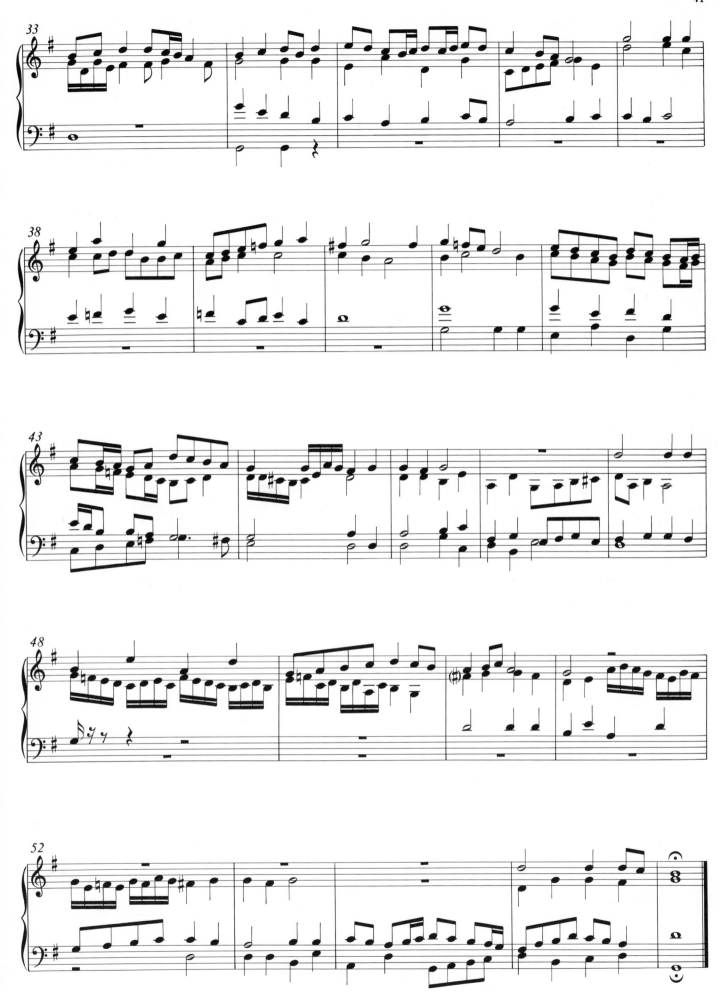

[43] Fuga in F

[44] Fuga in A

[45] Fuga in G

[46] Fuga in G

[47] Fuga of the second tone in G

[48] Fuga

Sign[or Johann Jakob] Froberger

[49] Fuga in A

B[ernhard] Meyer

[50] Fuga in A

[51] Praeludium in G

[52] Praeludium in G Minor

[53] Praeludium in E

[54] Praeludium in G Minor

[55] Praeludium in E

[56] Praeludium in E

[57] Fuga of the ninth and tenth tones in D

[58] Fuga in D

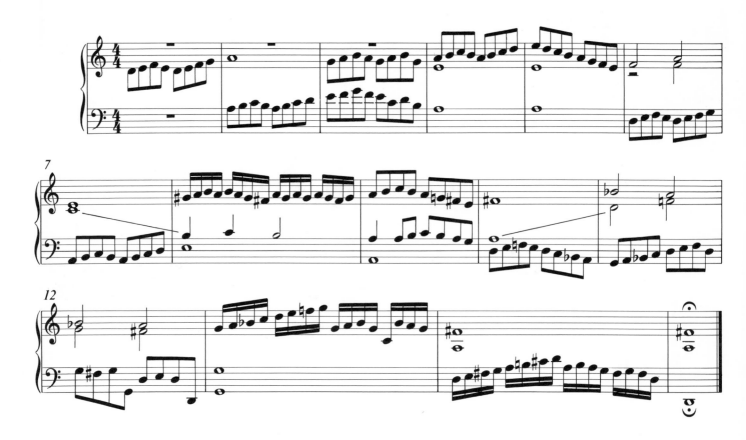

[59] Fuga of the third and fourth tones in A Major

[60] Fuga in G

[61] Fuga in D

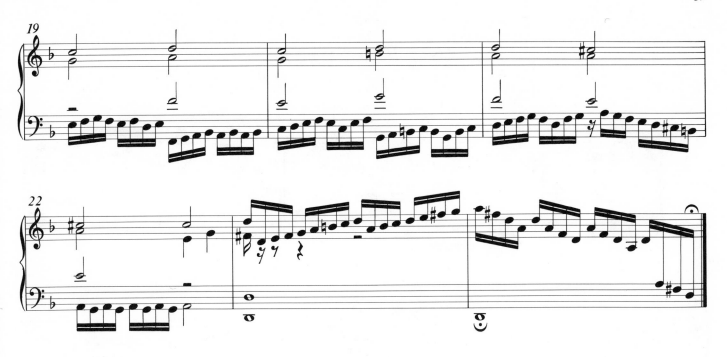

[62] Fuga of the seventh and eighth tones in C

[63] Fuga in D

[64] Fuga in A Minor

[65] Fuga of the second tone in D Major

[66] Fuga in G for February 1

[67] Fuga in D

[68] Fuga in G

[69] Toccata in D

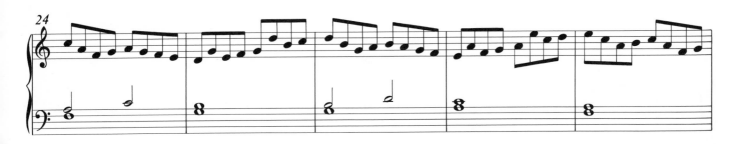

[70] Toccata in G

[71] Toccata in C : ''the fifth of February''

[72] Toccata in E

[73] Toccata of the second tone in G

[74] Toccata of the third tone:
"Durch Mordantam"

B[ernhard] Meyer

[75] Fuga Simplex of the third Mode

B[ernhard] Meyer

[76] Fantasia in G

[77] Principium of the eighth tone in G Major

[78] Magnificat: Intonation of the fourth tone in E

[79] Magnificat: Verse 1 of the eighth tone in G

[80] Magnificat: Verse 2 in G
Chorale in discant with two keyboards

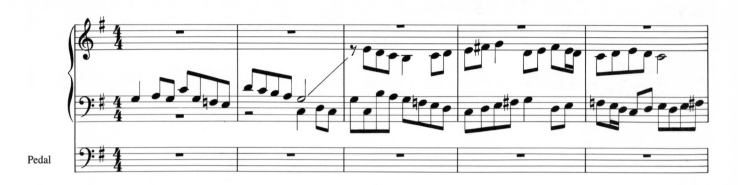

[81] Magnificat: Verse 3 in G

[82] Magnificat: Verse 5 in G
Chorale in Bass

Pedal

[83] Magnificat: Verse 6
Tutti

[84] Fuga in E

Dan[iel] Cron[er]
November 20, 1684